BRATZ™

Puppy Love

By Molly D. Leibovitz

SCHOLASTIC INC.

New York   Toronto   London   Auckland   Sydney
Mexico City   New Delhi   Hong Kong   Buenos Aires

ISBN-10: 0-439-91948-7
ISBN-13: 978-0-439-91948-7

Designed by Jenn Martino

12 11 10 9 8 7 6 5 4 3 2 1   7 8 9 10/0

Printed in the U.S.A.
First printing, January 2007

Chapter 1

Yasmin's room looked like a giant Valentine had exploded all over it. There were pink, red, and white balloons, streamers, confetti, lots of glitter, and giant paper hearts everywhere. She couldn't have been happier! With her three best friends, Cloe, Jade, and Sasha, Yasmin was planning what was sure to be the most fabulous Valentine's Day dance in the history of Stiles High!

"So you guys really think these hot-pink balloons are the way to go?" Yasmin asked, holding up a sample from a pile of balloons in an assortment of Valentine's Day shades.

"Absolutely," Jade replied. "It's totally hot!"

"Yeah, that's why they call it hot pink," Cloe teased. Yasmin tossed the balloon lightly at her friend's head, laughing.

"Okay, so I think I have plenty of inspiration here to set a fabulously gorgeous scene for the dance," Jade said.

"Really?" Sasha teased. "I wouldn't have thought there'd be enough to choose from." She gestured at the mounds of decorations surrounding them.

"I just wanted to make sure we had lots of options!" Yasmin said defensively. Yasmin was chairing the dance committee, with Jade handling decorations, Sasha choosing the music, and Cloe in charge of refreshments. But even though Jade was an expert at creating totally cool looks, she just hadn't been feeling completely inspired on how to create a fresh theme for this year's dance. Yasmin had picked up tons of ideas and called an emergency meeting to get it all figured out.

"I'm totally glad you did," Jade said. "I finally have a vision for this dance. It'll be all black and white polka dots, accented with hot-pink ruffles. It'll be classic, chic, and totally hip!"

"Sounds like my kind of dance!" Cloe replied.

"So, Cloe, you're making your famous cupcakes and yummy punch, right?" Yasmin asked.

"Of course! It wouldn't be a party without them!" Cloe loved turning everything, from her outfits to her bedroom, into a work of art. She loved baking because it gave her a chance to show off her artistic flair in a totally tasty way! Her cupid cupcakes were guaranteed to be the most divine ever. "I thought about adding to the menu, but then I realized everyone would be way too busy dancing to Sasha's hot grooves to eat, so I figured I'd keep it light."

"You're so right!" Sasha said. "I have the hottest playlist ever lined up for this dance — it's totally jammin', but also way romantic, since this is a Valentine's Day dance, after all!"

"I can't wait to hit the dance floor!" Jade said. "And Dylan's running the DJ booth?"

"Yeah — I was gonna do it, but I didn't want to cut into my dance floor time," Sasha replied. "And Dylan loves being in the DJ booth — he says it's the perfect way to scope out the whole room. Plus, girls come up to him all night and tell him how awesome his music is, which he totally loves!"

Their friend Dylan loved to be the center of attention, so playing DJ was perfect for him because he got to be front and center!

Yasmin slumped back against the pile of cushy pillows propped on her bed. "I am so relieved that everything's finally coming together!"

"Yas, you know this will be the coolest dance of the year," Sasha reassured her.

"How could it not be, with the four of us in charge?" Cloe chimed in.

"True," Yasmin agreed. "The whole school seems to be totally pumped about it—I think we're actually gonna sell out of tickets!"

"That's awesome!" Cloe said. "Ohmigosh, I am so excited about this dance!"

"And the most exciting part is yet to come," Jade added.

"Hmm, what could that be?" Sasha asked, grinning.

"Picking out our outfits, of course!" Jade exclaimed.

"Of course," Sasha replied. "So, Yasmin, are we ready to move this committee meeting over to the mall?"

"Let's do it!" Yasmin said. The dance was only two weeks away—she couldn't believe they still hadn't picked new dresses! They all loved to come up with spectacular new styles, but they'd been so busy planning the dance that they hadn't had time to plan their outfits for the night.

The girls piled into Cloe's cruiser and jetted over to the mall. They were strutting down the walkway, headed for Unique Boutique, one of their fave shops, when they heard a familiar voice calling their names. They turned to see their friend Vinessa heading toward them. They hadn't known her as long as they'd known each other, but she was super-nice and they were thrilled to see her.

"Hey, Vinessa!" Jade exclaimed. "We were just about to pick out our outfits for the Valentine's Day dance. Wanna join us?"

Vinessa looked uncomfortable, twirling a lock of her shiny platinum blond hair around her finger and staring off into space. "I don't know..." she said.

"It's okay," Sasha said, "we totally understand if you already have plans."

"It's not that," Vinessa replied, fidgeting with the strap of her cute striped messenger bag. "It's just that I don't think I'm going to the dance."

"You have to go!" Yasmin cried. "I've been planning it forever, and it's going to be amazing!"

"I'm sure it'll be wonderful," Vinessa replied. "But . . . " she looked down at her cute peep-toe

wedges and sighed. The other girls exchanged worried looks—this didn't sound like the cheerful girl they knew!

"Vinessa, what's wrong?" Cloe asked.

"Well . . ." She paused again, tugging nervously on her sparkly baby-T before finally admitting, "I don't have a date for the dance."

"Oh, is that all?" Cloe looked relieved. "I thought it was something really horrible!"

"But it's Valentine's Day," Vinessa moaned. "The most romantic day of the year! And I can't even get a date!"

"I'm sure you could get one," Sasha replied, shaking her head. "But why would you want one? We think Valentine's Day is the perfect opportunity for a totally awesome girls' night!"

"That sounds really fun," Vinessa said. "But the thing is, I've never had a Valentine for Valentine's Day. I've never had someone send me flowers, or chocolates, or even a card. Well, except my parents and my friends, of course."

"So you want a special someone to send you presents, huh?" Cloe asked, looking thoughtful. The other girls exchanged looks again—they could tell their friend was cooking up a scheme!

"It'd be nice, just this once," Vinessa replied. "So I'm really sorry, but I'm just having trouble getting psyched about this dance."

"You really should come with us," Jade said. "We'll have a fabulous time."

"I'm sure," Vinessa agreed, "but I really don't want to go unless I have a date. I wanna have someone to dance with, you know?"

"But we'll all dance together!" Jade insisted. "We always go to school dances in a big group, and we always have a blast!"

"You don't have to decide now," Yasmin interrupted, seeing how uncomfortable Vinessa looked. "Just promise you'll think about it—and that you'll come shopping with us right now!"

"That I can do!" Vinessa agreed, looking relieved.

"Then let's go!" Jade exclaimed. The girls strode into Unique Boutique and got down to some serious shopping.

Chapter 2

The girls hit the racks, giggling and squealing with excitement at each fabulous new find. Jade headed straight to the Betsey Lederhosen section. Betsey was a hot, new designer, and Jade was one of the first to start wearing her clothes. Jade found a black-and-white patterned wrap dress that was silky, hip, and just her size!

Meanwhile, Cloe was flicking through a skirt rack. She pulled out a hot-pink skirt with pretty, sparkly beads sewn all over it. Then she picked out a sweet little lace-trimmed cami to try on with it.

Sasha was busy burrowing through the trendiest clothes in the store. She had an armful of sleek black miniskirts and cherry red tops. And Yasmin was poring over racks of creamy-colored dresses. But one poofy pink dress caught her eye—it wasn't her usual taste, but she couldn't help it, she loved it.

In the dressing room, the girls oohed and ahhed as each came out of her booth, showing off one stylin' outfit after the next.

When Jade showed off her black and white slip dress, her friends gave her a big thumbs-up.

"That dress looks amazing on you, Jade!" Sasha told her.

"It's a new Betsey Lederhosen," Jade replied. "And I'm totally in love with it!"

Sasha was next, strutting out of her dressing room in a flared black skirt with ruffles at the bottom and a cute little tank top. Cloe followed, holding up one top after another, to go with each of the skirts she was trying.

Finally, Yasmin and Vinessa emerged from their rooms, Yasmin decked out in a fabulous, golden cocktail dress that came down to her knees in a little flare, and Vinessa in the poofy pink dress Yasmin had found.

The girls had a hard time narrowing down what they wanted to buy. The Bratz tried to limit themselves to outfits for the dance. But, of course, there were so many cute things that each girl ended up with one or two items that would be perfect for school or a weekend outing.

When they regrouped, Vinessa, Cloe, Jade, Yasmin, and Sasha compared their finds.

"Sasha, I love that little pink top you got," Jade said. "You're so stylin'."

"And that ruffled turquoise skirt that Cloe got is going to look awesome with her new boots," Yasmin added.

"Hey, Vinessa, I love that glam ensemble you put together," Jade said. "That dress is going to look so chic with that beautiful new barrette. I can't wait to see how it all looks together."

"As always, Jade, you've picked out the most spectacular look of all," Cloe declared.

"We're all gonna look amazing at the dance," Sasha replied.

Vinessa just looked down at the floor, and kept very quiet.

"C'mon, let's hit the smoothie bar!" Yasmin said, trying to cheer her up.

The girls ordered their favorite smoothie

flavors and settled in around a table with shopping bags all around them. From the number of bags, it was obvious the trip had been a huge success.

"I can't decide which new outfit to wear to the dance," Yasmin complained. She didn't want to make Vinessa feel bad, but she was so excited that she couldn't stop planning for the dance!

"I totally love your cute new polka-dotted dress," said Cloe. "It'll go perfectly with the dance decorations!"

"Yeah, I think that's the one I'll wear," Yasmin agreed. "You know, our new looks are so sweet, everyone's gonna want to be our Valentines!"

"I'm crazy about my outfit too," Vinessa said. "Too bad I don't have anywhere to wear it."

The girls had convinced Vinessa to grab some new threads, because you never know when you might need a totally cool ensemble! But now it seemed like Vinessa was even more bummed that she wasn't going to the dance.

"I have an idea," said Yasmin. "Why don't you join the planning committee for the dance? You can help us make it fabulous, and you'll be totally involved. Then you'll have to come!"

"That's really sweet," Vinessa replied, "but I think it would make me feel even worse to be that involved in a dance I'm not even going to."

"Are you sure?" Yasmin asked. "You could help with whatever you want — decorations, food, music, anything. I know we'd have tons of fun planning the dance together!"

"I'm sure it would be totally fun," Vinessa said. "I mean, I always have the best time hangin' with you girls, so why should planning a dance be any different? But I don't think I'd be any fun, with as down as I am about this whole Valentine's Day thing."

"We totally understand," Sasha said. "But we hate to see you so sad! And it really will be a fantastic party... promise you'll at least think about it."

"Valentine's Day really is the perfect time to celebrate fabulous friend- ships!" Cloe added.

"I'll think about it," Vinessa agreed.

"And if you change your mind about the planning committee, the offer's always open," Yasmin said.

Vinessa looked at her watch. "Oh no! I was just supposed to drop into the mall to pick up this new eyeshadow I've been wanting, but shopping with you girls is so much fun that I totally lost track of time! Now I've really gotta jet."

"Hope we didn't make you too late!" Jade said.

"No, I had an awesome time," Vinessa replied. "I'm so glad I ran into you girls!" She quickly scooped up all of her shopping bags and gave the girls a little wave. "See you at school tomorrow, 'kay?"

"Bye!" the girls chorused. They watched their friend walk away, then got down to serious business.

"Wow, she is so totally bummed," Jade said.

"I know—I wish there were something we could do to cheer her up," Sasha agreed.

Cloe looked around at her friends, and slowly a smile spread across her face. "I think I might have the perfect plan," she said. "If a date is what it takes to give Vinessa a happy Valentine's Day, then we'll just have to get her a date!"

Chapter 3

The next day at school, the girls hit the halls on a mission. They'd decided there was no way they were letting their friend sit home alone on Valentine's Day. If the only way to get her to the dance was to find her a date, then that's exactly what they were going to do. They were sure they could convince one of their guy friends to take Vinessa to the dance. Usually they all went in a big group, but the girls were sure that one of the guys would be happy to have a sweetie like Vinessa as his date. They'd gotten to school early so each of the girls could work on one of their closest guy friends. By lunchtime, they hoped to have a Valentine lined up for Vinessa!

Cameron, Eitan, Koby, and Dylan were all hanging out by their lockers when the girls strolled up.

"Perfect!" Cloe whispered to her best friends. "Let's get 'em!"

"But remember, we have to make them think it's their idea to ask her to the dance," Sasha reminded them. Then, louder, she said to the guys, "What's happenin', boys?"

"Nothin' much," Dylan replied, leaning against his locker. "Just trying to decide which of our slick new looks to wear for the Valentine's Day dance." Dylan was almost as into style as the girls were, and was always sporting super-hip looks.

"Did you guys go shopping this weekend too?" Cloe asked excitedly. "I can't believe we missed you at the mall!" She shot a look at Cameron, and he grinned back at her shyly. Their friends exchanged grins—those two were so into each other, but they would never say so out loud, because they didn't want to mess up the awesome group of friends they all had going.

"Yeah, we picked up a couple things," Dylan replied. "We're gonna look so hot, you'll have to give us some extra space on the dance floor so you don't get burned!"

The girls laughed and shook their heads at Dylan's corny line. But that was Dylan—he was fast-talking and always totally sure of himself.

"I'm sure you'll all look great," Yasmin agreed.

"You'll be happy to know that we'll be lookin' pretty cute too."

"No doubt," Eitan replied.

"Well, thank you," Yasmin said, lowering her eyes modestly. "But you know, I was wondering if there's anyone, you know, special you'd like to hang out with the night of the dance?" She tossed back her long brown hair and looked at Eitan expectantly.

"Ummm . . . I think all you girls are pretty special," Eitan said, looking confused.

"That's true!" Jade interjected. Yasmin shot her a look, and Jade put her hand over her mouth, gesturing for her friend to keep going.

"That's really sweet of you to say, Eitan," Yasmin said, "but is there maybe somebody in particular you'd like to go to the dance with?"

"Um, I'm, um, not sure," Eitan stammered,

starting to get flustered. "Wh-why do you ask?" He backed up, moving away from Yasmin ever so slightly.

"Just curious," Yasmin replied. "Because I know someone who'd totally go with you." Yasmin was sure that if she kept dropping hints, she could convince Eitan to ask Vinessa to the dance. But he didn't seem to be catching on.

"Who's that?" Eitan asked, starting to feel less confused and more intrigued.

"She's a really sweet girl, and an awesome friend," Yasmin began, but Eitan cut her off.

"Yasmin, if you want to go to the dance with me, you know you just have to ask!" Eitan said. "There's no reason to beat around the bush!"

Yasmin's face turned scarlet and felt so hot that she thought it might melt. "Don't be embarrassed," Eitan said. "I mean, I really wanted to just go in a group, but I'll go with you if you really want."

"I wasn't asking you!" Yasmin cried. "I—I've gotta drop by the newspaper office before class. I'll see you later." She hurried off, mortified, while the others watched.

"Dude, what'd you do this time?" Koby asked Eitan.

"I don't know!" he exclaimed. He looked around at the other girls for help. "Can anyone explain to me what I did wrong there?"

"Don't worry about it," Sasha replied. "I'll tell you later." Shaking his head, Eitan headed off down the hallway. With the way this day was going so far, he figured it couldn't hurt to be a little early to class.

In the meantime, Cloe had been working up the nerve to talk to Cameron. Part of the problem was that, even though she was totally psyched to hit the dance with all her girls, she was secretly hoping that Cameron might ask her to the dance. But she would never admit that out loud. Ever. And besides, they were all friends, so what was the big deal? Whether he went with Vinessa or just with the group, they were all sure to have an awesome time hanging out together. So Cloe took a deep breath and marched over to Cam, determined to help Vinessa out.

"Hey, Cameron," she said softly.

"Hey, Cloe," he replied. He glanced at her shyly, then quickly looked away.

"So are you still going to the dance?" she asked.

"Of course!" he replied. "Aren't you?"

"I have to go — I'm in charge of refreshments!"

Cloe said. "So I'm going to be really busy all night, making sure everyone gets plenty of cupcakes and punch. But you — you can do whatever you want!"

"Do you need help with the refreshments?" Cam asked. He wasn't sure what Cloe was getting at.

"No!" Cloe said. "That's not what I meant at all! I just meant that, you know, you could go to the dance with the whole group, or take a date, or not even go at all, if you wanted."

"Why wouldn't I go?" Cameron asked.

"I'm just saying, if you wanted to take the opportunity to maybe spend some time with someone you don't know that well, I think that'd be an awesome thing to do for Valentine's Day," Cloe explained. "You know, it's good to get to know someone new every once in a while." Cloe began to twist a lock of blond hair around her fingers, nervously.

"Whoa. You don't want me to hang out with you guys at the dance?" Cameron looked hurt.

"No, it's just—we always go to the dance in a big group," Cloe continued, "and I just thought you might want to go with a date, for once."

"Hey, I could get a date if I wanted one," Cam snapped. "I thought we all wanted to go together, but fine—if you don't want me to come with you, maybe I just won't go at all!"

"No—" Cloe cried, trying to think of a way to dig herself out of this mess. She couldn't understand how Cameron had so totally misunderstood her!

"Forget it, Cloe!" Cameron said angrily. "I just won't go, okay?" He stalked off as Cloe watched in horror. Her lips clamped shut so tightly they turned white as she tried to hold back her tears.

"Ohmigosh, now Cameron totally hates me," she moaned.

"It's okay, Angel," Sasha said, putting her arm around her friend. Cloe's friends all called her Angel because she was such a sweetie—and because she tended to have her head in the clouds! "We'll explain everything to him at lunch, okay?"

Cloe nodded, sniffling. Sasha gave her friend a quick hug, then turned her attention to Koby.

"So, Koby, do you know anyone who'd like to take a good friend of mine to the dance?" she asked. She'd decided to take the direct route, because hinting around clearly hadn't worked for her friends!

"Whoa, I am not taking Cloe to the dance!" Koby said, looking from Sasha to Cloe nervously. "No offense, Cloe, but Cam would never forgive me!" Cloe was still brushing away her tears, and Koby looked terrified. "Hey, no hard feelings, okay? But I've really gotta go!" And he dashed off, leaving the others staring at his back.

Jade had been chatting with Dylan, asking him about his plans for the dance. But Dylan had overheard his friends' conversations, and was now sure he knew what was going on.

"Girls, girls, I think I know what you're getting at, and there's really no need to get all worked up," he said. "I'd be happy to escort all of you lovely ladies to the dance—four dates isn't too many for the Fox!" Everyone called Dylan the Fox because of his smooth-talking style.

Jade, Cloe, and Sasha stared at Dylan, then burst out laughing.

"What?" Dylan asked. "What'd I say?"

"Okay, that is so not what's going on here," Jade said, once she'd caught her breath enough to talk again. Dylan totally cracked her up!

"Well, if that's not it, then what's the deal?" Dylan asked.

"You know our friend Vinessa, right?" Sasha said.

"Sure," Dylan replied. "She's a total sweetie. I wouldn't mind getting to know her better!"

"Okay, perfect!" Cloe exclaimed. "That's exactly what we were hoping one of you boys would say."

"See, Vinessa really wants a date for the Valentine's Day dance," Sasha explained. "So we thought we'd get one of you guys to take her. We had no idea our little plan would turn into such drama!"

"Ohhh," Dylan said. "So none of you were trying to ask any of us out?"

"Not for ourselves!" Cloe said. "We were trying to set Vinessa up with one of you."

"Sure, I'll go with her," Dylan said with a shrug.

"You know what?" Jade said. "I really don't think this whole matchmaking thing is a good idea. Thanks for the offer, Fox, but let's just go in a big group like we planned."

"Works for me," Dylan agreed. Dylan was always willing to go with the flow, which was part of why the girls loved to hang with him.

"Will you explain to the guys what we were talking about, though?" Cloe asked worriedly.

"No prob," Dylan replied. Just then, the bell rang, and they all scattered in a mad rush to get to class on time.

Chapter 4

Cloe, Jade, Sasha, and Yasmin strutted into the lunchroom and staked out their usual table. Soon, Dylan strolled up to join them, with Cameron, Eitan, and Koby trailing behind.

"Oh man, I hope they're not still upset," Cloe said worriedly. Just then, Cam took the seat next to her, and she flashed him a nervous look.

"Cloe, I'm so sorry I totally freaked out earlier," he said. "Dylan explained everything, and I know you were just trying to help out a friend. It really did sound like you were trying to ditch me, though!"

"I know—I thought I was being subtle, but I know I was just totally confusing. Sorry I messed it up so badly."

"No worries," Cameron said. He and Cloe shared a smile, relieved not to be fighting anymore.

"Cloe, I'm sorry too," Koby said. "I'd totally go to the dance with you if you wanted, but Dylan told me it wasn't you Sasha was talking about at all!"

"And, Yasmin, I shouldn't have assumed you were trying to ask me out," Eitan added. "I mean, I know if you really wanted to, you'd just ask straight out!"

"True," Yasmin said with a grin. "Though it is traditional for the guy to ask the girl . . . "

Eitan looked worried, and Yasmin exclaimed, "Just kidding! I am totally not trying to ask you out."

"Besides, we don't have to wait around for someone to ask us out," Sasha added. "We're independent women!"

"Yeah!" the girls chimed in, giving each other high fives.

Then Jade turned to Dylan. "Isn't there anything you wanted to say?"

"Hey, thinking all you girls wanted to hit the dance with the Fox was a totally natural mistake," Dylan replied. The girls all groaned, and

Jade tossed a straw wrapper at his head. "What'd I say?" Dylan asked, giving them an innocent look.

"Okay, now that we're all cool again, I have an exciting announcement about the dance," Yasmin said.

"What is it?" Cloe asked eagerly.

"Hey, I thought we were all in this planning thing together," Sasha said, pretending to be offended. "I can't believe you have dance news we don't know about!"

"Well, after I left this morning, I dropped by the newspaper office and saw that we're doing a front-page story on a totally awesome pet rescue group called Have-a-Heart," Yasmin began, "and I thought it would be really cool if the dance could be a fundraiser, so we could do something good while having a totally fabulous time!"

"Sounds good to me," Jade chimed in.

"So I called Have-A-Heart, and they were totally pumped about the idea," Yasmin continued. "I even got the newspaper story changed to say that proceeds from our Valentine's Day dance will raise money for the group!"

"Great job, Yas!" Sasha exclaimed.

"And what's even better is they're going to bring some of their puppies to the dance, so people can see the sweet little pets they're helping—and adopt one on the spot, if they want!" Yasmin smiled happily at her friends' excited reactions.

"That's so cool!" Cameron said.

"I know!" Yasmin agreed. "They just have to bring written permission from their parents, and they can take a puppy home with them that night!"

"Oooh, and puppies are totally lovable, so they're

perfect for a Valentine's Day dance," Cloe squealed.

"This really is gonna be the best dance Stiles High has ever seen," Sasha declared.

"Wow, I'm totally gonna ask my mom if I can adopt a puppy," Eitan said.

"I'm totally getting one too," Dylan added. "I'd love to have a cute li'l puppy to run around with!"

Yasmin was totally thrilled that her friends were into her idea. She was really excited that their super-fun dance could also help some pets find fantastic new homes. And she figured everyone would be happy to have some cute puppies to hang out with if they got tired of their dates!

"Now I really can't wait for the dance!" Cloe cried.

Chapter 5

"Now we have to get Vinessa excited about this dance," Jade said that afternoon. The girls were all hanging out at Cloe's house, working on their homework and talking of course, always talking. "She really can't miss it now — it's gonna be so cool!"

"Yeah, but getting her a date was a total flop," Cloe sighed. "So how are we ever gonna convince her?"

"I say we plan the most fabulous girls' night ever," Jade said. "If we make it truly spectacular, she won't be able to resist!"

"You're right," Yasmin agreed. "We could spend all day at the spa, get ready together, and take a limo over to the dance."

"That sounds perfect," Sasha agreed.

"I'll book manies and pedies at the Stylin' Salon 'n' Spa," Yasmin said.

"Oooh, why don't we get our hair and makeup done there too?" Cloe asked.

"Do you really think they can do a better job than we can do ourselves?" Jade teased.

"No . . . but it's fun to get pampered, anyway," Cloe said. "And I bet they could manage to do a decent job."

"Probably," Sasha agreed. "Hey, while you're at it, book us some massages too!"

"Totally," Yasmin agreed. She whipped out her glitzed-up cell phone and dialed the spa, where she booked a day full of appointments for massages, manis & pedis, and makeup and hairdos for five. "Just in case we can tempt

Vinessa with all the fabulous primping we have planned!"

"I know, I can't wait," Sasha said, fantasizing about getting totally pampered before the dance.

"I have another idea to really put things over the top," Cloe added. "Let's plan the coolest, girliest slumber party in history for the night of the dance. We can all sleep over at my house after the dance!"

"That sounds amazin'! We can play truth or dare, bake brownies, tell scary stories, and give each other makeovers. It'll be awesome!" Jade exclaimed.

"It'll be the perfect end to the perfect dance," Yasmin added.

Cloe called Vinessa to tell her about their new plan. The Bratz were on a mission to cheer Vinessa up!

"That does sound fabulous," Vinessa agreed. "What if I hit the spa with you, then meet up with you at your place after the dance? Then we'll still get to hang out, but I can skip the dance itself."

"That's silly!" Cloe cried. "All that primping would go to waste!"

"You're right," Vinessa agreed. "Well, can I still come to your sleepover, even if I don't join you for the rest of the day?"

"Of course!" Cloe agreed. "But I swear it will be an awesome time."

"I know, and it really means a lot to me that you girls want me to go," Vinessa replied. "But Valentine's Day really bums me out, and I don't wanna bum you out too!"

"Hey, and I don't wanna be bummed," Cloe said with a laugh. "But I'm sure we could cheer you up if you'd let us!"

"I'll think about it," Vinessa promised.

Cloe hung up and sadly shook her head at her friends. "She still won't come," Cloe said.

"Okay, then, we just haven't come up with the

right plan yet," Sasha declared. "I'm not giving up till we get that girl to come out with us on Valentine's Day!"

"Yeah!" her best friends agreed.

"But what else can we do?" wondered Yasmin.

"What if one of us calls her and pretends to be a boy and asks her to the dance?" Jade suggested.

"I don't think any of us sounds enough like a boy to pull it off. And anyway, eventually we'd have to come up with an actual boy — so it still wouldn't help," Sasha pointed out.

"Yeah, I guess you're right," Jade admitted. "But there's got to be something we can do."

"Well, what if we left her notes," Sasha said slowly. "You know, maybe from a . . . a secret admirer or something? That'll add a little romance to her Valentine's Day!"

"Not bad, Angel. I'm running the Have-a-Heart-Grams table for the dance, so I could totally send her some," Yasmin said.

"Wait, what-a-what-grams?" Jade asked.

"Have-a-Heart-Grams. You know, special Valentine's Day messages that people can send each other at school," Yasmin explained. "We're selling them to raise money for the Have-a-Heart charity. Sorry, girls, did I forget to tell you about that part?"

"Yes, but we'll forgive you because it's such a totally awesome idea!" Sasha replied. "And I know just what to write."

Cloe pulled out a large pad of drawing paper and some markers from her desk, and Sasha started writing:

Dear Vinessa,

Roses are red
Violets are blue
You're so pretty
and I like you.

- Your Secret admirer

P. S. Let's meet at the
Valentine's Day dance!

"Sasha, that's perfect!" Yasmin squealed. "But who are we gonna have meet her at the dance?"

The girls looked at each other nervously. Then Sasha replied, "Well, Dylan did agree to take her. If nothing else, he can meet her there."

"True," Jade agreed. "But we better let him know he's sending secret messages first!"

"Girls," Yasmin interrupted, "that sounds like

a plan, but if we don't finish this math homework, Mr. Gonzales is gonna be sending us secret 'you failed' messages."

"We need studying music!" Sasha said. She flipped on Cloe's CD player, and they all turned back to their math books, busily scribbling down answers as they bobbed their heads in time to the music.

Chapter 6

The next day at lunch, Yasmin was running the Have-a-Heart-Gram table, and the line to buy one stretched all the way to the back of the cafeteria! Cloe had used her amazing artistic abilities to design flyers that they had put up all over the school, plus the decorations for the booth in the cafeteria. Now everyone just had to buy a Have-a-Heart-Gram for all their friends or crushes.

"We're raising so much money for those sweet

homeless pets!" Yasmin squealed excitedly to Cloe, who had joined her at the booth because there were way too many people for Yasmin to help all by herself.

"Did you send that special note yet?" Cloe whispered.

"It's the first one that went out today," Yasmin confirmed with a wink. The grams would be delivered in the first class after lunch every day until the dance. The girls couldn't wait to see what Vinessa would think of her first note from her secret admirer!

After school, Vinessa ran up to the Bratz in the parking lot, and they could see right away how excited she was from her sparkling eyes and her flushed cheeks. "Guess what!" she exclaimed.

"What?" Yasmin asked innocently. Sasha aimed a quick wink at Jade and Cloe.

"You'll never believe it!" Vinessa cried.

"C'mon, tell us!" Cloe prodded. "I can't stand the suspense!"

"I have a secret admirer," Vinessa announced.

Sasha, Yasmin, Cloe, and Jade all smiled at Vinessa and tried hard to look surprised. They could barely disguise their delight.

"Really?" Jade asked. "Who do you think it could be?"

"Was there a note in your locker?" Sasha asked.

"Well," Vinessa began, "I actually got a Have-a-Heart-Gram. I have it right here in my pocket. You can read it!" Vinessa pulled the crumpled piece of heart-shaped pink paper out of the pocket of her jeans.

The four girls clustered around Vinessa to check out the Have-a-Heart-Gram.

"Oooooh, how romantic!" Yasmin murmured. Suddenly, she was starting to feel a little bit nervous. "So are you going to go to the dance?" she asked.

"Oh my gosh, how could I miss it?" Vinessa squealed. "It would mean I'd never find out who my secret admirer is. I couldn't stand him up! Wow, I wonder who it could be?"

"Yeah, I wonder . . . " Cloe's voice trailed off, her thoughts whirling.

"The dance is going to be amazing!" Vinessa said. "It'll be my first Valentine's Day date ever — and with a totally romantic secret admirer!"

"We're so excited for you, Nessa," Jade

murmured. Her stomach was starting to do somersaults.

Uh-oh, Sasha thought.

"Well, I guess I'll be seeing you at the dance after all!" Vinessa said, and she turned to go, practically floating from excitement.

"Oh no, guys . . . are you thinking what I'm thinking?" Sasha began.

"What will happen when Vinessa gets to the dance and discovers that there is no secret admirer? She's gonna be so upset," Yasmin cried.

"We're in big trouble," Jade said.

"Well, we're just going to have to think of a way to fix it," Sasha said sternly. "I mean, Vinessa is expecting something truly spectacular. Dylan is awesome, but he's not exactly romantic. I don't think he'll pass for a way-sweet secret admirer."

"Then who will?" Cloe asked. The girls all stared off into space.

"I've got it!" Yasmin shouted finally.

"What? What is it?" the others asked eagerly.

"Well, remember how the Have-a-Heart charity is bringing all those pets to the dance? Well, what if we adopted one of those Have-a-Heart puppies for Vinessa?" Yasmin suggested.

"And he could be her Valentine!" Cloe chimed in.

"Exactly!" Yasmin agreed, smiling.

"Vinessa does love dogs," Jade added.

"Let's do it!" Sasha exclaimed. "We'll give her an awesome Valentine's Day after all!"

Chapter 7

"First, we have to get her parents' permission," Sasha said. "Then we'll head over to the Have-a-Heart shelter and pick out a sweet little puppy that's just right for Vinessa!"

"Perfect!" Yasmin, Cloe, and Jade exclaimed.

The four girls followed Vinessa as she made her way down the street, away from Stiles High.

"Ssshhh, we have to be sneaky," Sasha warned the others. "She can't know we're following her."

The girls tailed Vinessa to the mall entrance.

"Perfect, she's going shopping!" Yasmin squealed.

"Probably for a dress to wear to the dance . . . to impress her secret admirer!" Cloe moaned.

"At least we know she's not home," Yasmin said, "so we can go talk to her parents right now."

"Great," Jade said, "let's go!"

The four girls headed straight over to Vinessa's house.

"Here goes," said Cloe.

When Vinessa's mom answered the door with a smile, the girls all jumped in to explain their plan.

"I don't know if you've noticed, but Vinessa's been totally bummed about Valentine's Day—" Cloe began.

"And we've tried to cheer her up, but nothing's worked—" Jade continued.

"And at the Valentine's Day dance, we're raising money for a pet rescue group—" Yasmin interjected.

"So we wanted to know if we could adopt a puppy for her, and it would be waiting for her at the dance!" Sasha finished.

"It'll be her very own Valentine," Cloe added.

"That is so sweet of you girls," Vinessa's mom said. "I wondered why she'd been moping around this past week. And to think, it was all because of a dance! But if this can cheer her up, I'm all for it."

"Will you write us a permission slip so we can adopt the dog for her?" Sasha asked.

"Sure," agreed Vinessa's mom, turning to grab a pen and paper. "She's been asking for a pet forever, so this will be perfect." She wrote quickly and handed the slip of paper to the girls. "Pick out a really cute puppy for us, okay?"

"The cutest!" Jade agreed. The girls waved good-bye as they hurried down the front steps.

"That was so easy," Cloe said. "What a relief!"

"But we still have to find the right dog for Vinessa. That won't be as easy as it sounds," Yasmin warned.

"Then we better get goin'!" Sasha declared, and the girls headed over to the Have-a-Heart shelter.

* * *

The girls strode up to the front door of the Have-a-Heart shelter and could immediately hear the barks and meows of the animals inside. They knew it would be totally hard to choose just one! Inside, they were greeted by a kind-looking old lady.

"Mrs. Engel?" Yasmin asked. When the woman nodded, she continued, "My name is Yasmin, and I'm organizing the Valentine's Day dance at Stiles High."

"Of course," said the woman. "We're so thrilled

about the fundraiser you're doing with us." She paused, looking at the girls. "You aren't canceling on us, are you?"

"Oh no!" Yasmin cried. "We actually wanted to adopt a puppy in advance, to be presented to one of our friends at the dance."

"And it's okay with her parents?" Mrs. Engel asked.

"It sure is!" Sasha replied, holding out the piece of paper from Vinessa's mom.

"Then, please, come take a look around!" said Mrs. Engel. "I'm sure you'll find a puppy your friend will love."

The girls trooped inside, and each immediately sighed with delight. There were dozens of dogs all over the room, lounging on sofas and chairs, cushions and rugs. They all looked super-cute, but soon the girls spotted an extra-cute little brown and white spotted puppy that was rolling around on his back.

"Hey, you guys, look at this one. He's adorable!" Sasha pointed to the small, roly-poly puppy.

"Oh my gosh, he's perfect!" Cloe cooed. She made her way across the room and knelt down beside the tiny puppy. She stroked his back and gently ran her fingers along his velvety ear. Enjoying the attention, the puppy happily licked her hand. "What a sweetheart!"

"You might even call him a Valentine!" Yasmin said.

"Wow, I think I'm in love," Sasha murmured as the friendly little pup scampered over to her and climbed into her lap, where he licked her on the nose! The puppy's ears were long and floppy and super-soft. His fuzzy coat was shiny, and his little black nose was wet.

"I think we've found just the right puppy," Yasmin told Mrs. Engel.

"Oh, he is a sweet one, isn't he?" the woman said. "We just found him — he doesn't even have a name yet! But he's definitely ready for a brand-new home."

"Now he has a name and a home!" Yasmin said. "We're gonna call him Valentine!"

* * *

The girls took turns carrying the little puppy in a special plastic carrying case that had lots of air holes in it.

As they headed home, Jade thought of an important detail. "Wait a second, guys!"

"What is it?" Cloe asked.

"Where is this sweet li'l guy gonna spend the night?"

The girls looked at each other, shocked that they hadn't thought of that before.

"Hey, I have an idea . . . what about Dylan's pad? He was talking about how he wanted a puppy to play with, and I'm sure his parents wouldn't mind," Cloe said.

"Perfect!" Yasmin exclaimed. "I'll call Dylan right now."

Dylan agreed to watch the puppy for the night, and the girls hurried over to his place.

On the front porch, Jade pulled Valentine out of the pet carrier and cradled him in her arms. Dylan opened the door right away, and as soon as he saw the puppy, a huge grin stretched across his face.

"Is this the little guy?" he asked.

The girls all nodded.

Dylan reached out to take the puppy, and Valentine immediately licked him on the nose.

"Dylan, meet Valentine," said Sasha.

"He's our Valentine's Day present to Vinessa," Cloe said. "He's gonna meet her at the dance and be her Valentine!"

"That's so cool!" Dylan exclaimed as the puppy wriggled and squirmed in his arms. "Do you want me to bring him to the dance for you?"

"That would be perfect," Yasmin agreed. "Because we'll have a lot of setting up to do."

"I'll take good care of him and have him there lookin' sharp tomorrow night," Dylan said.

"Thanks, Fox!" Jade said. The girls ambushed him with a quick group hug, with Valentine at the center.

Chapter 8

"Hey, Nessa!" Cloe greeted her friend. Now that she had a secret admirer, Vinessa had agreed to meet her friends at the Stylin' Salon 'n' Spa. The day of the Valentine's Day dance had arrived, and it was time to get ready. The girls were totally psyched to start the preparations with full-on pampering at the spa. Then they would head over to Cloe's house to finish getting ready for the dance.

"Hey, girls," Vinessa replied. She looked so happy she was almost glowing. "I can't wait to get my hair and nails done. It'll be so relaxing."

"You're gonna look fabulous!" Cloe added.

"We're glad you came with us," Yasmin said. "Now let's get this spa party started!"

They strolled into the salon and settled into the oversized, comfy chairs while soaking their feet in warm tubs of bubbly, soapy water. Scented candles burned nearby, and soothing instrumental music played softly in the background.

"This is wonderful," Sasha sighed. "I could do this every day."

"I wish," Jade said.

"Totally," Cloe agreed. "It's so relaxing."

"Something to look forward to when we're rich and famous!" Yasmin added.

They each picked out shades of pink and red

for their mani-pedies — Cloe went for the softest ballet slipper pink, Jade chose a hot magenta, Sasha picked a deep red, Yasmin selected a silvery rose, and Vinessa settled on fuchsia.

"I love that color on you, Nessa!" Yasmin exclaimed as they sat side by side while their nails dried.

"Well, that rose color is perfect for you, Yas!" Vinessa replied.

"It's so cool that we could choose colors from the same family, but each in our own distinctive shade," Sasha mused. "It's like our friendship — we have a ton in common, but we all have our own talents and interests too."

"Thank you, Professor Sasha," Jade teased.

"But seriously, you guys are awesome friends," Vinessa said. "And I just know we're gonna have a fabulous time at this dance!"

A whirlwind of hair styling and makeup followed, and soon the girls all looked totally glam. They were hanging out at the front of the spa, sipping green tea, when suddenly Cloe looked at her watch and gasped. "Girls, we have got to start getting dressed. The dance starts in two hours!"

The girls hopped into her cruiser and jetted over to her place. The totally hot outfits they had picked out were lined up in Cloe's room, along with tons of shoes and accessories they had all brought to share and swap.

"I love all our new outfits," Cloe squealed. "We're definitely gonna turn some heads tonight!"

"As always," Jade interjected.

"But we haven't seen your outfit yet, Vinessa," Yasmin said. "What are you gonna wear?"

"I'm actually not sure," Vinessa said nervously. "After I found out about my secret admirer, I went back to the mall and got a pretty new dress, but I'm just not sure if it's right."

"Well, let's see it!" Sasha exclaimed.

Vinessa stepped into the bathroom to change, then reappeared in an elegant pale-pink sheath dress paired with silvery ballet slippers. She did a little twirl in front of the mirror, then turned to her friends to see their reactions. "Well? What do you think?"

"You look incredible!" Yasmin exclaimed.

"Your secret admirer is gonna be blown away!" Jade added happily.

The girls touched up each others' up-dos, adjusting bobby pins and adding pretty, sparkly barrettes to glam up their hairstyles. They added a little lip gloss and accented their looks with glitzy necklaces, earrings, and bracelets.

Finally they all looked perfect, and it was a good thing, because it was time to go!

They grabbed their beaded, satiny handbags and dashed outside, where a white stretch limo was waiting to take them to the dance.

"Wow," Vinessa sighed. "I've never been in a limo before!"

"Oooh, you are in for a treat!" Sasha said.

The girls climbed into the back of the limousine, each looking gorgeous in her own unique way. The fridge in the back was stocked with yummy juices, and the seats were totally cushy and comfortable.

"I think I might be starting to like Valentine's Day!" Vinessa exclaimed as the limo pulled away from the curb and carried them off to the dance.

Chapter 9

The girls pulled up at the dance and stepped out dramatically like they were strutting down a catwalk. "Come on, girls, we have a lot of work to do before the party gets started," Yasmin said.

Inside, Sasha queued up her playlists at the DJ booth and made sure the speakers and lights were all set up just right. Cloe grabbed the punch and cupcakes from the kitchen and set them out, making sure they looked totally perfect. Jade put up a few more streamers and balloons, and sprinkled confetti on the tables around Cloe's refreshments. "Fabulous!" Jade declared.

Yasmin was flailing around, making sure everyone was ready so they could greet their classmates in style. She helped Mrs. Engel and her volunteers set up the puppies around the room. Everything seemed to be going perfectly, but then she noticed that Vinessa was standing off to the side of the room, tugging at her dress anxiously. "Guys, I'm so nervous." Vinessa's voice shook ever so slightly. "I mean, what if my secret admirer doesn't show up? What if I—what if I get stood up? I'll just die of shame!" She looked around the room as though searching for something, then gasped, "Or what if I don't like him? What if I'm stuck with a totally boring date all night?"

"Don't worry, Nessa!" Cloe reassured her friend. "I just know he'll be here, and I know you'll have a spectacular night."

"I don't know . . ." Vinessa said uncertainly.

"Cloe's right, Vinessa," Jade said, coming up beside Vinessa and putting her arm around her friend. "This is gonna be an amazin' Valentine's Day!"

"Promise you'll stay with me until I find my secret admirer?" Vinessa asked, grabbing Cloe's hand.

"Of course we will! That's what friends do!" Cloe promised. She led Vinessa to the top of the stairs, where Yasmin, Jade, and Sasha were waiting for them. From there, they could see the whole party—and it looked spectacular!

The whole room sparkled in glittering hearts, accented with chic black and white polka dots.

Perfectly cut fuchsia and silver hearts fluttered from the ceiling, and hot-pink and white streamers were draped from the walls. Pink strobe lights lit up the dance floor, while tables laden with punch bowls and adorable pink and white cupcakes, each with a little figurine of cupid balanced delicately on top, filled the back of the room. The dance floor was totally packed with all the students from Stiles High showing off their smoothest moves.

"Wow," Cloe gasped, "I've never seen a more dazzlin' party!"

"Then let's get out there!" Sasha exclaimed. The girls sashayed down the stairs while Vinessa kept looking around nervously. The girls had never looked better, and they knew it! It was time to hit the dance floor.

Jade elbowed Sasha, who turned and nudged

Yasmin, who tapped Cloe on the shoulder. It was time to introduce Vinessa to her furry new secret admirer.

Cloe looked around for Dylan and saw him hanging out with the other guys by the DJ booth. She gave him a wink, which he returned with a wide grin.

"He's bringing Valentine over now," Cloe whispered to Yasmin.

The Bratz watched as Dylan pulled Valentine's cardboard crate out from under the coat check table. But when he looked inside, his eyes widened in shock, and he gestured desperately for the girls to come over.

"What's going on?" Jade whispered.

Cloe shrugged helplessly. "I have no idea, but we're about to find out."

"Hey, Dyl, what's up?" Cloe asked quietly. She checked to make sure Vinessa wouldn't overhear, but luckily she was too busy scanning the dance floor to pay attention to what they were saying.

"Um . . . " He looked around uncomfortably, his brow wrinkling. "Um, Cloe, can I talk to you?" He paused for a second. "Privately?"

"Uh, sure, I guess so." Cloe looked at Jade, who looked puzzled. Cloe just shrugged and followed Dylan away from the group of girls.

"Dylan, what's going on? Where's Valentine?"

"Um, I'm not sure how to tell you this, but I seem to have, uh, well, I seem to have lost Valentine." Dylan looked down at the floor, then raised his eyes to meet Cloe's. "I mean, we got here, and he was in his crate and seemed totally fine. But, just now when I went to bring him over to you, the crate was empty! I have no idea where he went. I'm so sorry, Cloe. But he's got to be here somewhere, right?"

"Right. We just have to find him," Cloe declared. She whirled to scan the dance floor for the tiny puppy, but the dance floor was so packed that she couldn't see anything.

Cloe ran to grab the girls and explained what had happened. "So we've gotta save Valentine before he gets trampled!"

The girls headed for the dance floor, but suddenly Cloe cried, "Wait, where's Vinessa?"

"She decided her secret admirer might be too shy to come up to her in a big group, so she wanted to go off by herself for a little bit," Jade explained.

"Well, we've gotta find that puppy before she finishes circling the room," Sasha said. "Let's hit it, girls!"

"Okay," Yasmin said. "Let's enlist the guys to help us search the room. We've gotta fan out and each check a different area."

"I'll hit the refreshment table," Cloe said. "Maybe he's trying to nab some goodies!"

"I'll check the DJ booth," Sasha offered.

"I'll grab the guys, and we'll search the dance floor," Jade said.

"And I'll keep Vinessa distracted so she doesn't start to wonder what's going on," Yasmin said.

"I know we'll find Valentine before Vinessa knows anything happened," Cloe said.

"What can I do to help?" Dylan asked worriedly.

"Just keep spinnin' those tunes," Sasha said. "We've gotta keep this party goin' while we find that puppy."

"You're not mad at me, are you?" Dylan asked. "I feel so bad that I lost Vinessa's new puppy."

"Of course not—it's totally not your fault," Jade reassured him. Then she wove her way to the center of the dance floor, grabbed Cam, Eitan, and Koby, and shouted something over the music. They all split up to search the dance floor, squeezing between the crowds of dancing teen-agers.

Yasmin went to find Vinessa and couldn't help but wonder—where could that rascally little puppy have gone? And would they ever find him in time?

Chapter 10

"I can't believe I got stood up for a dance I didn't even wanna go to," Vinessa moaned. "Maybe I should just go home."

"Aw, c'mon, the night is still young," Yasmin replied. "I'm sure he'll be here any minute. But in the meantime, why don't we get a little dancin' in?"

"Well, this is a good song . . . " Vinessa said.

Yasmin grabbed her friend's arm and pulled her onto the dance floor, where they were soon jammin' with the rest of the crowd.

"Awesome moves, Vinessa!" Yasmin called over the music. Just then, she spotted the guys scouring the dance floor, and she whirled Vinessa around so she wouldn't see them.

"Check out Dylan burning up those turntables," Yasmin said. "Doesn't he look slick?"

"He is kinda cute," Vinessa agreed. "You're friends with him, right?"

"Totally!" Yasmin replied, grinning. Maybe Vinessa didn't need a secret admirer after all! Yasmin kept moving around to block Vinessa's view of the dance floor, while her friends searched desperately for the missing puppy.

The girls were started to get really worried. They had searched everywhere, but there was still no sign of Valentine. They met up with the guys in a corner to try to see if anyone had found any clues.

Just then, Jade noticed the coat check right next to them. "Ohmigosh, we forget to check in there!" She ran over to the coat check area, where tons of cool coats were hung from every rack. The room was so packed with coats that some had even slipped off their hangers and into piles on the floor. Jade waded through the cluster of coats, peering into every corner, until she spied a furry little form at the back of the room.

"Valentine, is that you?" she asked. She headed for a faux fur coat that lay crumpled on the floor. Once she got close, she could see a cuddly brown and white puppy curled up on top of it, snoozing. He snored softly, and his legs twitched as he dreamed a happy little puppy dream.

"There you are, little sweetie," Jade sighed. "C'mon, boy, let's go meet your new friend Vinessa!"

She scooped up the puppy, who woke up and immediately started licking her fingers, making her giggle.
As soon as she stepped back out onto the dance
floor, her friends spotted her carrying the puppy
and crowded around.

"I'm so glad
you found him!"
Cloe cried.

"C'mon, let's
get this puppy
over to Vinessa,"
Sasha said.

"Wait," Jade
said, "I think Dylan
should be the one
to present him to
Vinessa."

"Good idea, Kool Kat," Cameron agreed. Jade's friends all called her Kool Kat because she was the coolest! "Dylan would be totally into taking the spotlight."

"Aww, he's so cute and cuddly!" Eitan said, stroking the puppy's ears.

"Okay, let's get him to the DJ booth," Jade said. She and Sasha headed over, while the others went to distract Vinessa.

"Where'd you find him?" Dylan gasped when he saw the girls approaching with Valentine.

"He was dozing in the coat closet," Jade explained.

"You silly puppy!" Dylan exclaimed. Jade handed the puppy over, and Dylan cradled Valentine in his arms.

"Dylan, why don't I take over the DJing duties for a minute," Sasha suggested.

"Hey, I thought I was doing an awesome job," Dylan complained.

"Oh, you are, as always," Jade replied. "But we have a very important job for you."

"We need you to present the puppy to Vinessa," Sasha explained.

"I mean, who better than a cute guy like you to make her Valentine's Day complete?" Jade said.

"That I can do!" Dylan said, running his hand through his carefully styled hair.

Sasha switched on a sweet romantic tune while Dylan strode over to Vinessa. Jade trailed after him, but she couldn't help but wonder — would Vinessa's secret admirer be everything she'd been hoping for?

Chapter 11

"Hi, Vinessa." Dylan said, holding Valentine behind his back as their friends gathered around. "Happy Valentine's Day!"

Vinessa stopped dancing and turned to face her friends. "Happy Valentine's Day, Dylan," she said softly.

"Are you having fun tonight?" Dylan asked.

"I am . . . but, well, I'm a little disappointed," Vinessa replied.

"Disappointed?" Eitan exclaimed. "But this is the hottest party of the year!"

"No, it is — I mean, you girls all did an amazin' job," she told her friends, "but, well, I was supposed to meet my secret admirer tonight, and he totally stood me up."

"No he didn't," Dylan said with a big smile.

"Wait! Is it . . . " Vinessa looked at Dylan with surprise.

"Here he is!" Dylan exclaimed, pulling the puppy from behind his back and holding him out to Vinessa.

"Aww, what a cutie!" Vinessa cooed.

"This is your Valentine," Yasmin explained. "And he's been waiting to meet you all night!"

"This is my secret admirer?" Vinessa asked in disbelief.

"We knew how bummed you were about Valentine's Day — " Jade began.

"And we couldn't figure out any other way to get you here," Sasha continued, "so we made up a secret admirer."

"Please don't be mad!" Cloe said.

"Mad?" Vinessa asked, cuddling her new puppy. "How could I be mad when I have the sweetest Valentine ever?"

"We're so glad you like him!" Yasmin exclaimed.

"You know, this has been an awesome day," Vinessa said. "I'm so glad you girls wouldn't let me skip it. You're totally right that Valentine's Day is the perfect time to hang with your best friends!"

"Not to separate you from your Valentine, but, Vinessa, may I have this dance?" Dylan asked, sounding shy for probably the first time ever.

"Totally!" she agreed. Yasmin held the puppy while Dylan and Vinessa danced, and soon their other friends were groovin' all around them. Then Sasha flipped on a totally hot playlist, and hit the dance floor with her friends. They were all jammin' to the music, trying out hip new moves, when suddenly the principal interrupted, tapping the microphone at the DJ station.

"Ahem," said the principal. "Ladies and gentlemen," he began.

"You guys, listen up," Yasmin said, shushing her friends, who were still chattering and giggling happily.

"I'd like to thank you all for coming out to this

Valentine's Day dance," the principal continued, "but most of all, I'd like to thank our Yasmin, who put together this whole event, along with Jade, Sasha, and Cloe. Not only did these girls plan this whole event, but they also raised a lot of money for the Have-A-Heart animal rescue charity. And I'm pleased to report that all of the puppies the group brought here tonight have now found new homes!" The room burst into applause and cheers, and the girls stepped forward to take a bow.

"And now it's time to announce the new Valentine's Day Have-a-Heart Queen," the principal announced. He pulled a large white envelope decorated with pink hearts from his coat pocket, and opened it with a flourish. He pulled out a red card with gold printing and held it up. "I am happy to introduce your very own Stiles High Have-a-Heart Queen, Vinessa!" The students all cheered wildy, chanting Vinessa's name.

"Now are you glad you came?" Jade teased.

"Congrats, girl—you deserve it!" Sasha said.

"Now get up there!" Cloe said, giving her friend a playful push.

Vinessa hurried to the front of the room, and the principal placed a sparkly tiara on her head.

"I just wanna thank my amazin' friends Cloe, Jade, Sasha, and Yasmin," Vinessa said into the microphone. "Girls, come up here and share the spotlight!" The girls ran up to join her, and they shared a big group hug.

"Now it's time for your first dance as the official Have-a-Heart Queen," the principal announced. "Who's the lucky guy who gets to dance with you?"

"Actually, I'd like to share this dance with my best girls," Vinessa said. "After all, they're the ones who made this the best Valentine's Day ever!"

The girls looped their arms around each others' shoulders and swayed to one of their fave tunes. "Wait, something's missing!" Vinessa exclaimed.

"What's wrong?" Cloe asked worriedly.

"I need my Valentine out here with me!" Vinessa motioned Dylan over and took her puppy from him, then kept dancing with Valentine cradled in her arms.

"So you enjoyed your Valentine's Day ?" Jade asked.

"This was seriously the coolest day ever," Vinessa said.

"And it's about to get cooler," Cloe said. "Because we're about to head to the most spectacular sleepover in the history of sleepovers!"

"Awesome!" the girls exclaimed.

Chapter 12

"Good night, boys!" Cloe, Jade, Yasmin, and Sasha called out to Dylan, Cameron, Koby, and Eitan.

"Happy Valentine's Day, Cam," Cloe said shyly as she waved good-bye.

"Dylan, you can come over and play with Valentine anytime you want," Vinessa told her friend.

"Really ?" he asked.

"Absolutely!" Vinessa replied. "Valentine would love to see you anytime—and so would I." She and Dylan shared a smile as the puppy licked Dylan's hand.

The five girls linked arms and walked back to their fabulous limo.

"This has been such an incredible night," Yasmin sighed.

"And I can't wait to chill with you girls back at my place," Cloe said.

"What are we gonna do?" Vinessa asked.

"Oh, the usual—makeovers, chick flicks, maybe a little gossip . . . I think we'll keep ourselves busy!" Jade announced.

At Cloe's house, the girls hopped out of the limo and headed straight to Cloe's bedroom, where five sleeping bags in pinks, purples, greens, and blues were laid out, waiting for them.

Cloe set out a plate of yummy cupid cupcakes, while Yasmin popped a bowl of popcorn, and Sasha carried in some cold sodas.

"Well, girls," said Jade, holding up a can of soda for a toast, "here's to a fabulous night."

"To a fabulous night," the others echoed, and they all clinked soda cans.

"To the best Valentine's Day ever!" Cloe added.

"And to the best friends a girl could have!"

Vinessa said. She scoped out the cupcakes and said, "Mmm, I've gotta try one of those!" Valentine squirmed out of her arms and tried to grab one too.

"Looks like no one can resist your cupcakes!" Sasha told Cloe.

"Oh, I bought some puppy food, if the little guy's hungry," Cloe said, pulling out a cute hot-pink dog bowl filled with puppy chow.

"You girls thought of everything!" Vinessa exclaimed.

"We do try," Jade said modestly.

"So who's up for a movie?" Yasmin asked.

"I am!" the girls chorused.

"Before we pop in a DVD, there's something I want to say," Vinessa interrupted. She pulled the sparkling crown off her head and held it out to her friends. "This crown is really for you guys.

Without you, I'd never have gone to the dance, and I'd never have realized that the very best way to celebrate Valentine's Day is to spend it with your girls. You're the greatest friends ever, and I can't thank you enough for giving me Valentine, and showing me how special this holiday is, and how special our friendship is. So, thank you!" She gave a queenly curtsy, and the girls giggled.

"We're always happy to help," Sasha said.

"After all, that's what friends are for!" Yasmin added.

"Now let's get into our PJs and get this girls' night started," Jade said. The girls changed quickly, then sprawled out on their sleeping bags as one of their fave chick flicks started to play.

"Let the slumber party begin!" Jade proclaimed.

"Girls, I totally love Valentine's Day," Vinessa said, smiling at all of her friends.